Oswald was still weak from his ordeal but he managed to struggle up on to one elbow. 'Mistress Villiers, I bring news from the army in the north ... We were driven from the field, beaten like dogs at a place called Naseby.'

Wherever this place was, Edward knew that the King's army had suffered a terrible defeat.

'What of His Majesty, Oswald? Does the King live?'

Oswald nodded. 'God be praised, they say he is fled to Oxford and I wish him well, though many as fought for him weren't so lucky.'

Alice was almost afraid to ask the next question. 'And our father, what of him?'

Oswald could not meet her eye. 'I'm sorry, Miss,' he said at last ...

Children of the New Forest

Captain Marryat

Retold by Peter Tabern

Based on the Childsplay Television
Series for BBC TV

PUFFIN BOOKS

PUFFIN BOOKS

Published by the Penguin Group
Penguin Books Ltd, 27 Wrights Lane, London w8 5tz, England
Penguin Putnam Inc., 375 Hudson Street, New York, New York 10014, USA
Penguin Books Australia Ltd, Ringwood, Victoria, Australia
Penguin Books Canada Ltd, 10 Alcorn Avenue, Toronto, Ontario, Canada m4v 3b2
Penguin Books (NZ) Ltd, Private Bag 102902, NSMC, Auckland, New Zealand

Penguin Books Ltd, Registered Offices: Harmondsworth, Middlesex, England

First published 1998
3 5 7 9 10 8 6 4 2

Puffin Film and TV Tie-in edition first published 1998

Copyright © Peter Tabern, 1998
All rights reserved

The moral right of the author has been asserted

Set in 12.75/17pt Monotype Baskerville
Typeset by Rowland Phototypesetting Ltd,
Bury St Edmunds, Suffolk
Made and printed in England by Clays Ltd, St Ives plc

British Library Cataloguing in Publication Data
A CIP catalogue record for this book is available from the British Library

isbn 0–141–30263–1

In memory of Richard Cooper
1930—98

Contents

1 High Keeper of the King's Forest   1

2 News of War   5

3 Jacob Armitage   8

4 The Levellers   12

5 The Cottage in the Forest   19

6 A New Life   23

7 Roundheads   27

8 Trapped   34

9 A Wild Goose Chase   41

10 Pablo   47

11 Alone   55

12 Smoke and Fire   61

13 Under Arrest   67

14 Turbary Bower   73

15 Night Visitors   80

16 The Treasure Chest   85

17 Prisoners   89

18 King's Mill   95

19 When the Moon is Full   100

20 A King's Reward   107

21 To the Death   112

22 A New Beginning   118

One

High Keeper of the King's Forest

Aʀɴwood house in the New Forest was not the sort of place you would ordinarily expect to find a king. But these were not ordinary times. The year was 1645, England was torn by civil war and Charles Stuart was only too pleased to spend a night under Squire Beverley's roof. And if by morning the Squire was ready to join his army and bring along plenty of gold for the royal war chest, so much the better.

Before he rode off with the King, Squire Beverley lined up his children in the courtyard and said goodbye to them. There were four Beverley children and, since their mother died, they had been looked after by their aunt, Judith Villiers, but the truth of it was they were too much for her and they often ran wild.

This morning, however, they looked as though butter wouldn't melt in their mouths and only the servants knew what a struggle it had been to make them all so clean and presentable.

Edward, who was fourteen, wore a dove-grey velvet doublet, a lace collar and black silk breeches, and looked every inch the Lord of the Manor's eldest son. His brother and sisters were also wearing their finest clothes. Alice, thirteen, wore a gown of watered silk. Humphrey, aged eleven, looked very smart in his plum-coloured velvet jacket and even little Edith, the baby of the family at eight years old, had a new dress of the purest white linen. Her long blonde hair had been set in grown-up ringlets but still she couldn't help crying when her father kissed her goodbye.

'Now, now, little missy,' he said gently, 'no tears. You must do your duty and make your father proud.'

Squire Beverley had a special word for each of them, and at last he came to Edward.

'Remember, my boy, while I'm away everyone will look to you. You stand in my place. You make the decisions, understand?'

'Yes, Father. I won't let you down.'

'No, I know you won't.' The Squire took hold of

the boy by the shoulders and looked steadily into his eyes. Then from inside his glove he took a gold crucifix on a chain and placed it in his hand. 'Will you wear it?'

Edward nodded and his look said that he would wear it always. Then, with a fanfare from the royal trumpeter, King Charles himself appeared, flanked by his favourite courtiers, the Lords Tarleton and Bressingham.

Everyone bowed low and the King was about to mount his horse when Squire Beverley coughed politely and pointed to Edward.

'Sire, last night you were gracious enough to promise . . .'

'Ah, yes,' said the King, 'it is your wish that we honour your son?'

'It is, Sire.'

'And you, boy,' said the King, 'are you ready for this honour?'

'I am, Sire,' said Edward nervously.

The King raised his hand for silence. 'Edward Beverley, do you swear lifelong allegiance to your sovereign, Charles, by the Grace of God Defender of the Faith, King of England, Scotland, Ireland and sundry lands beyond the seas, as long as your heart beats and there is breath in your body?'

'I do, Sire,' gulped Edward.

'Then, when it shall please God to call your father to Himself, we do name you High Keeper of the King's Forest in his place, to keep our laws and preserve our peace.'

The King laid his hand briefly on Edward's head, the trumpeter blew another fanfare and all the men rode off to war, the King and his courtiers in front, the Squire and his foresters behind.

Squire Beverley turned at the gates and waved his plumed hat, the children waved back and then he was gone. And that was the last time they ever saw him.

Two

News of War

THE WEEKS PASSED AND a great chill descended
on Arnwood. With all the able-bodied men away at
war, the house and grounds soon fell into disrepair and
Aunt Judith stayed more and more in her own room,
leaving the four children to their own devices.

Then one morning Edith was woken up by the
sound of a horse snorting and pawing at the cobbles
of the courtyard. The sound went on and on, echoing
about the house, and yet no one else seemed to have
heard it, so Edith wrapped a shawl about her shoulders and went to investigate alone.

The rider of the horse had been lying slumped
against the great front door and when Edith slipped

the bolt he fell backwards into the house and there he lay, clothes torn, his face a mask of blood and dirt. For a long moment Edith stared at him and then, very loudly, she screamed.

Servants came running and carried the injured man to the table in the great hall and soon everyone including Aunt Judith was gathered round.

Alice sponged away the blood and grime, and only then did they all realize that the mysterious rider was none other than Oswald Partridge.

'Well, Master Partridge,' said Aunt Judith sternly, 'what do you mean by frightening us all half to death?'

Oswald was still weak from his ordeal but he managed to struggle up on to one elbow. 'Mistress Villiers, I bring news from the army in the north . . . We were driven from the field, beaten like dogs at a place called Naseby.'

'Naseby?' said Aunt Judith. 'Never heard of it.'

Wherever this place was, Edward knew that the King's army had suffered a terrible defeat.

'What of His Majesty, Oswald? Does the King live?'

Oswald nodded. 'God be praised, they say he is fled to Oxford and I wish him well, though many as fought for him weren't so lucky.'

Alice was almost afraid to ask the next question. 'And our father, what of him?'

Oswald could not meet her eye. 'I'm sorry, Miss,' he said at last, and when he lay back there were tears in his eyes.

The children looked at each other.

'A pretty mess,' said Aunt Judith bitterly, 'four penniless orphans and an old woman left to shift for themselves. A pretty mess indeed!' And with that she turned on her heel and left the room.

Alice looked pale but her voice was calm and determined. 'Edward, you and Humphrey must go at once and find Parson Ratcliffe . . .'

'No, Miss,' said Oswald quickly, 'don't do that. Go and find old Jacob Armitage. He'll know what to do. Don't go to Parson Ratcliffe. It's too dangerous.'

'Why is it dangerous?' asked Edward.

'Your father was a King's man,' said Oswald, 'and Parson Ratcliffe was his friend. It's only a matter of time before the Roundheads come to take him.'

Three
Jacob Armitage

Later that morning, Edward and Humphrey took the track across the Lymington road to the part of the forest where Jacob Armitage lived.

Years ago Jacob had been head forester, but he had long since retired and Squire Beverley had allowed him to live anywhere he liked in the forest. It was Jacob who had chosen to go as far as possible from other people.

The villagers whispered that he had once had a wife and a daughter who had died of the fever and from that day on not another living soul had entered his cottage. Nowadays few could even remember where it was.

As the boys walked, Edward held his father's gold crucifix, still on its chain, and Humphrey – practical, good-natured Humphrey – followed a pace or two behind.

Edward was proud that his father had died fighting for the King. As far as he was concerned, that was how every soldier wanted to die, but Humphrey wasn't so sure.

'Dead is dead. Does it make any difference how?'

'Of course it does. Father was loyal and true and he did his duty. He died fighting the Round-heads.'

Neither Edward nor Humphrey had ever seen a 'Roundhead', the name given to the supporters of Parliament led by Oliver Cromwell.

The Roundheads were the King's enemies in the civil war. Roundheads wore their hair close-cropped, unlike the Cavaliers, who let their hair grow to shoulder-length, a style which both Edward and Humphrey copied. Humphrey's long hair was always getting in his eyes and now he pushed it back and squinted up at his brother.

'So what happens to us? Are we supposed to live with Aunt Toad Face for the rest of our lives?'

But Edward wasn't listening. He had heard something moving off to one side of the track and, silencing Humphrey with a warning finger, was already moving stealthily into the forest.

In no more than ten paces the undergrowth thinned into a small clearing and there, tethered to a tree, Edward found a sturdy brown New Forest pony, and across its back the carcass of a freshly killed deer.

Edward looked about him for the owner, but the forest was deathly still. Not even the song of a bird broke the silence. Then, very close, he heard the unmistakable click of a musket being cocked.

'You're dead, boy,' said a low voice, 'you and your brother along with you.'

Edward found himself staring down the barrel of a gun and into a pair of pale blue eyes the colour of cold steel. He had found Jacob Armitage.

Jacob Armitage was perhaps sixty years old, which in those days was a very great age, yet he still seemed as strong and unyielding as a forest oak. His face was lined and weatherbeaten to the colour of shoe leather and he had a long beard and silver-grey hair. He had served the Squire as head forester for many years and had even taught Edward to hunt, so when the boys told him their father was dead a look of real sadness clouded his face.

'Oswald Partridge told us to come and find you,' said Humphrey.

'You're lucky you didn't find a troop of Round-heads,' replied Jacob, and when the boys looked at each other in disbelief, he told them that Roundheads had already been seen in the forest.

'Your father trusted Parson Ratcliffe,' said Jacob. 'We must seek him out and ask his advice, if the Roundheads haven't beaten us to it.'

Four

The Levellers

JUST AS JACOB FEARED, it was already too late. That very morning a dozen troopers, dressed in sober black and grey, iron-helmeted, face-guards barred like prison windows, had ridden down the Lymington road and made their way straight to Parson Ratcliffe's church. The parson, however, had already fled into the forest with his daughter, Clara, taking any objects of value he could carry from the church.

The Roundheads were led by a preacher, a man called Abel Corbould, who was not in the least surprised to find that the priest had run away and did not waste time searching the empty church. Instead he ordered his men to round up the local villagers and bring them to the churchyard.

When they were all assembled, Corbould climbed on to one of the tombstones and gave them the speech he kept for such occasions.

'People of Arnwood, we bring you good news! We are of the Leveller persuasion and we hold that no man should set himself higher than his fellows.'

Corbould's wild blue eyes scanned the crowd and the villagers shuffled uneasily.

'The Lord has sent us to deliver you from your oppressors. No more shall this church deceive you or its pulpit pour forth lies.'

At a signal from their sergeant, William Hammond, the Levellers carried the wooden pulpit from the church to where a pile of brushwood had been laid among the gravestones.

Corbould smiled at the people. He was no more than nineteen or twenty and had grown a thin beard to make himself look older. In fact, it did the very opposite; it made him look like a child, a dangerous child to be sure, but a child in man's clothes.

Hammond set fire to the brushwood and soon the flames were licking at the pulpit steps. Other troopers brought pictures and hangings from the church and the villagers watched in silence as these were added to the fire until the flames roared and the smoke rose high above the steeple.

Jacob and the boys saw the smoke while they were still some way off and at once Jacob left the track so they could approach cautiously under cover of the forest. By the time they were close enough to see what was happening, the bonfire was blazing with such a crackle that Abel Corbould had to shout to make himself heard.

'Cursed be men like Parson Ratcliffe who come ween you, the people, and your God! And cursed be the grandees like the Beverleys of Arnwood who beat the people to pieces and grind the faces of the poor!'

Edward and Humphrey looked at each other.

'Fear not, brothers and sisters, only give us their names, tell us where they are hidden, and they shall all be punished!'

'Is he talking about us?' asked Humphrey.

'Come on,' whispered Jacob. 'I think we've heard enough.' And he led the boys back the way they had come.

Moving quickly, they travelled the remaining miles to Arnwood House, where Jacob went straight in to see Judith Villiers, but not until he had instructed the children to collect together as many of their belongings as they could carry and wait for him in the courtyard.

Aunt Judith was in her chamber, seated at the window, looking out over the estate that Squire Beverley had left in her care.

'A pretty mess, eh, Jacob Armitage?' she said without looking at him.

'There are Roundheads at the church, Mistress, looking for Parson Ratcliffe. I think they may come here.'

'You've seen them, I take it? What do you make of them?'

'Rough, unmannerly,' said Jacob, 'led by a young preacher, hardly older than Master Edward.'

'Very well,' Judith Villiers sighed, 'you may take the children to a place of safety.'

'May I indeed? And what about you?'

'I shall stay here and speak with these Roundheads.'

She was a stubborn woman and Jacob knew better than to argue, but could he really leave her here?

'Suppose the children won't go without you,' he said. 'What then?'

'They must,' said the old woman simply, 'you must persuade them.' And with that she turned to the window and would say no more.

*

As darkness fell on the forest, the children, led by Jacob Armitage, left Arnwood behind them and began the long journey to the old forester's cottage. Edith sat on the pony, surrounded by bundles and boxes, while the others walked alongside, lost in their own thoughts. Then all at once Jacob stopped so suddenly that Humphrey bumped into him.

'What is it? What's the matter?'

The old forester didn't answer but simply raised his hand, inviting them to listen. From a long way off, drifting through the canopy of the forest, came a strange sound. Unclear at first, they soon realized it was the sound of men's voices, singing a hymn or a psalm of some kind.

'Quick!' said Jacob, and, seizing the pony's reins, he led the animal straight into the undergrowth, almost unseating poor Edith in the process. The others followed, and no sooner had they hidden themselves than the Levellers appeared, riding in formation, with several of them carrying lighted torches. Now as they came closer it was possible to make out the words they were singing:

The Lord is both my health and light,
Shall man make me afraid?

Since God doth give me strength and might
Why should I be dismayed?

They all rode huge black horses except for Corbould, the preacher, whose horse was as pale and slight as the man himself. They streamed past the place where the children were hiding and disappeared in the direction of Arnwood, although their haunting psalm still rang in the children's ears.

'Where are they going?' asked Edith. 'What are they going to do?'

Everyone looked at each other but no one wanted to think about it.

'Come on,' said Jacob. 'We've still a long way to go.'

Edith had almost dozed off with the steady motion of the pony when something made her turn and look behind her. There in the distance, against the darkness of the forest, was an orange glow and a great pall of white smoke above the trees. The others turned to look.

'What is it?' asked Humphrey.

'It's Arnwood,' said Jacob grimly, his voice little more than a whisper.

Edward, his face hard and fierce, threw down the

bundle he was carrying and began to run back along the track towards the distant flames, but Jacob was too quick for him. He ran after him and held the boy fast.

'No, Master Edward! It's no use . . .'

And so there they all stood in the darkness, and the children of the New Forest realized that they were looking at Arnwood House for the last time.

Five

The Cottage in the Forest

T HEY WALKED ALL NIGHT and then at last, just as dawn was breaking, they came upon a clearing in a grove of ancient, twisted chestnuts, and there on the far side was a plain thatched building that could have been an old barn or even a cowshed.

As they got closer, they could see windows with shutters, deerskins stretched on frames to dry and a grey dog with a thick shaggy coat who ran barking to greet them.

'Quiet, Smoker,' said Jacob lifting Edith down from the pony, but the dog ran happily around them, barking and wagging his tail as Jacob went to tether the pony, leaving the children to take in their new surroundings.

'What is it?' whispered Edith, staring at the ramshackle cottage.

Humphrey shrugged. 'Jacob's house, I suppose . . .'

'Ours too, if he'll have us,' said Alice sharply. 'Come on, everyone carry something.'

So they picked up their things and followed her indoors. Only Edward stayed behind, staring in disbelief at the place they had come to. To think, the High Keeper of the King's Forest brought to this!

When Jacob threw open the shutters, it became clear that the inside of the cottage was no better than the outside. A thin layer of straw covered the earth floor, the ash-filled grate was black and cheerless, and on the table was half a stale loaf and a candle stub. All in all, it was a far cry from Arnwood.

'You stay here, boy,' said Jacob to an openmouthed Humphrey, and he led the girls up a rickety staircase to a couple of tiny bedrooms. In the smaller of the two, he pulled a strip of sacking from the window and let in the glimmer of sunlight that found its way through the branches of the chestnut tree outside.

The room was bare except for a wooden chest

and a narrow bed on which was laid a thin straw mattress. It was all quite clean but didn't look as though it had been used or even visited for a long time.

'You can sleep here,' Jacob told Alice, 'you and the little 'un.'

'Edith,' said Alice, putting an arm around her sister. 'Her name's Edith. Thank you, the room's . . . very nice.'

'It smells funny,' Edith whispered, loud enough for the old man to hear.

Alice nudged her sharply and glared.

'It needs a sweep,' said Jacob, who had thrown open the chest and was pulling out various homespun garments that Alice thought must once have belonged to his wife and daughter.

'Here,' he said, 'your clothes mark you as high-born. You'd better put these on.'

'And what about our things?' asked Alice. 'Shall we put them in the chest?'

Jacob shook his head. 'No, bring 'em downstairs. I shall have to burn them.' And with that he left the room.

Alice went to the window and looked out at the chestnut tree. She was trying not to cry and soon she felt a small hand slip into hers.

'The soldiers burned our house,' said Edith quietly, 'and now he wants to burn our clothes. Soon there'll be nothing left of us.'

And the two sisters held on to each other in the green-tinged gloom of their strange new room.

Jacob found clothes for all of them except Edward, who stared into the empty hearth and would not say a word. Jacob was worried about the boy. The children were alone in the world and he was not getting any younger. He needed Edward to help look after the others and do his share of the work. At last he sat down beside him.

'It isn't easy, this,' he said, 'not for any of us. I've got my own life out here, ways of doing things. I don't relish having the four of you around any more than you relish being here.'

Edward did not move or even give a sign that he had heard.

'Oh, I know this is a step down for the High Keeper of the King's Forest,' said Jacob, 'but we owe it to your father and your aunt to keep ourselves alive. If we let your brother and sisters come to harm, what's it all been for, eh?'

Edward's look gave nothing away but deep inside he knew the old forester was right.

Six

A New Life

At first the time in the Forest passed quickly, mainly because the children had so much to learn. Jacob taught Alice to bake bread and he taught Edith to milk the cow and then to churn the milk into butter. Humphrey collected eggs from the chickens then tended the vegetable patch while Edward, whom Jacob had already taught to hunt, chopped wood for the fire and even tried his hand at mending the thatch on the cottage roof.

They dressed like a forester's children. The girls brushed the ringlets out of their hair and Alice cut the boys' hair short, the way the villagers wore it. No one came near the cottage and the children kept well clear of the Lymington road, so that apart from old Jacob they never saw another living soul.

Then one day, after supper, when Humphrey and Edith had cleared the plates away, Jacob announced that in the morning he would cross the forest to seek out Oswald Partridge and trade for some supplies. These days Oswald was head forester and would know if the Levellers were still at large and if the children were in any danger.

'Will you find out about Aunt Judith?' asked Alice, who was still hopeful her aunt might be alive.

'Yes, if I can,' said Jacob, 'and you must all tell me what supplies we need.'

'Why can't we go with you?' asked Edith.

'Because it's not safe,' said Jacob. 'The forest may still be full of Roundheads, so you must stay here, little 'un. Make yourself useful and help Alice. Now then, Alice, what do we need?'

'Flour,' said Alice, 'lots of flour.'

'And salt,' said Humphrey. 'We used the last of it in the broth just now.'

'Powder and shot,' said Edward, 'and some nails if you can get them.'

'And what about you, little 'un?' said Jacob. 'Is there anything you need?'

'I don't *need* anything exactly,' said Edith, 'but if

you see anything nice, I'd be very glad to have it . . .'

'Would you indeed?' said Jacob, smiling. 'Then we shall have to see what we can do. Now then, the boys must help me with a little job or I shall have nothing to trade and none of us will have the things we need.'

Jacob went over to the hearth and kicked out the dying embers of the fire. Then, wrapping some sackcloth around his hands to protect them, he ducked under the wooden beam above the fireplace until he was standing inside the chimney. From there he passed out great haunches of venison, beautifully smoked by the cottage fire.

There were five in all and, when they were laid out on the table, Jacob wiped the soot from his hands and faced the children.

'In the old days, before this war started, the King paid his foresters' wages and he paid my pension, regular as the church bell. But things are different now. None of us has been paid in more than two years, so I don't reckon His Majesty would begrudge us a bit of venison to make up for it, do you?'

Dutifully the children shook their heads and then they helped Jacob wrap the meat in strips of cloth, ready to be loaded on to the cart.

*

The following morning at first light they all gathered outside the cottage to see Jacob off.

'What if anyone comes while you're away?' asked Edward.

'The girls can say they're my granddaughters, here because of sickness in the family. They must both think of names for themselves.'

'And what about Edward and me?' asked Humphrey.

Jacob thought for a moment, then he patted the haunches of venison neatly stacked behind him in the cart. 'I reckon if that old chimney of mine can hide the King's deer, it can hide the King's subjects.'

Laughing to himself, he called Smoker up on to the cart and drove away along the forest track, leaving the boys hoping that no one would come to the cottage and force them to hide up a chimney.

Seven

Roundheads

JACOB DROVE ALL MORNING and the sun was high above the trees by the time he reached Keeper's Cottage. The journey had tired him. In fact, these days everything seemed to take an extra effort and lately he'd been bothered by nagging pains in his chest.

Oswald's children, Molly and Robert, were playing outside when the cart drew up and Jacob called them to fetch their father while he began to unload the venison. Edward and Humphrey had thrown straw over it which Jacob was just about to push aside when a voice bade him 'Good day' and he found himself face to face with the Leveller preacher from the churchyard. Jacob's hands froze.

'I thought I had met all the foresters,' said the preacher, taking in Jacob's leather tunic, 'but I confess I do not recall your name.'

'The name's Armitage. Jacob Armitage. Master . . . ?'

'Corbould,' said the preacher, 'the Reverend Abel Corbould. Forgive me, Master Armitage, but you seem advanced in years for a forester.'

Jacob bristled. 'I am retired from service, but I keep my tunic and my title in honour of that service,' he said proudly, just as Oswald Partridge arrived.

'Ah, Master Partridge,' said Corbould, 'the very man. I have a commission for you. We must speak.'

'Do you want to speak now?' asked Oswald, glancing at Jacob's cart and guessing what lay beneath the straw.

'No, no,' said Corbould pleasantly, 'at your convenience. Come up to the house. Good day to you, brothers.' And with that he spurred his horse and rode off.

That had been a close call and Oswald Partridge let out a long, slow breath, but Jacob was too angry to care.

'Advanced in years!' He spat on the ground. 'I'll give him "advanced in years"!'

Oswald smiled at his old friend and clapped an

arm round his shoulders. 'Jacob, it's good to see you! What have you got for us?' He nodded at the cart.

'The usual,' said Jacob, pushing back the straw to reveal the venison. 'Where do you want it?'

Oswald looked around nervously. 'Better get 'em inside, quick. We've got an Intendant coming today . . .'

'Oh yes?' said Jacob. 'And what's one of them when it's at home?'

'Some Roundhead sent from London to tell us how to run things,' said Oswald. 'Still, makes a change from Corbould and his damned Levellers. You know he's the one that torched Arnwood?'

Jacob was hoisting one of the haunches on to his shoulder as Oswald spoke and a sudden pain in his chest caught him, forcing him to stagger against the cart.

'Jacob! Are you all right?' Oswald helped him lower the venison back on to the cart.

'Yes, yes, I'm all right . . .' Jacob took a deep breath and tried to master the pain. 'He burned Arnwood, you say?'

'Without a word of a lie,' said Oswald, 'burned it to the ground, with the children and the old lady inside, God rest their souls.' And he picked up two haunches and made his way towards the cottage.

Jacob stayed leaning against the cart and crossed himself, partly in memory of old Judith Villiers and partly to give silent thanks that folk believed the Beverley children were dead.

Edward and Alice had spent the morning collecting mushrooms and their walk had taken them right up to the Lymington road. They were about to cross when a cart came rumbling round the corner. Alice was all for hiding, but Edward thought it was a good opportunity to test their new disguises.

'We're supposed to be peasants. It'll just look suspicious if we hide.'

The cart was carrying a Roundhead family. There was a gentleman dressed in black with a sombre high-crowned hat, a young girl perhaps a year or two older than Alice, looking very demure in her white Puritan collar and plain bonnet, and an older woman, who might have been their housekeeper.

The girl was very beautiful, with green eyes and thick red hair and, as she passed by, Edward could not help staring at her. She returned his look and even gave him a quick smile, before lowering her eyes. Then the cart turned a bend in the road and Edward found Alice staring at him.

'Roundheads!' he said contemptuously.

But Alice had seen that look and now it was her turn to smile.

'What?' said Edward, blushing to the roots of his hair.

'I didn't say anything,' said Alice innocently.

'The only good Roundhead is a dead Roundhead!' said Edward crossly, knowing he'd been caught, and he marched off into the forest, leaving Alice still smiling to herself.

The new arrivals were Mr Heatherstone, his daughter, Patience, and Phoebe, their housekeeper. They had travelled by coach from Winchester to Lymington, where a cart had been sent to carry them the rest of the way.

Mr Heatherstone was the new Intendant, a governor sent by Oliver Cromwell to make the New Forest safe for Parliament. Mr Heatherstone had also been promised Arnwood to live in, but by the time he reached Winchester he heard that the house had mysteriously burned down.

He and his daughter were now to live at a much smaller place that had belonged to the local parson. As if this were not enough to put up with, who should step out of the parsonage to greet them but Abel Corbould.

Both Heatherstone and his daughter knew Corbould from London, though neither of them cared for the man and they were certainly not expecting to find him in the middle of the forest. But he was courteous enough and helped reach their belongings down from the cart. However, when Patience asked what he was doing here, he simply smiled his thin smile and told them he was doing the Lord's work.

'I hear Arnwood House burned down,' said Mr Heatherstone. 'That wouldn't be the Lord's work by any chance, would it?'

Corbould shrugged. 'There are times when an example must be made. We must show the people that we mean to set things right. But never fear, I'm sure you will find this place quite comfortable . . .'

'That's not the point,' said Patience. 'My father has been sent to bring peace to the forest.'

'Peace will come when we rid the place of Royalists,' replied Corbould. 'In fact, tomorrow I was planning to take our head forester and scour the countryside –'

'I'm sorry, you can't do that,' interrupted Mr Heatherstone. 'The foresters are under my authority and I cannot spare them for such a mission.'

Corbould's eyes narrowed. 'Cannot? Or will not?

You know there is a priest at large, a man who served the Beverleys. It is our duty to track him down.'

'It is *my* duty to get this forest working again,' said Heatherstone, 'and I need every serving man. Now, if you'll excuse us, Master Corbould, we have had a long and tiring journey. Come along, Patience, Phoebe.'

But Abel Corbould was not so easily put off. 'You say you need every *serving* man . . . Suppose I were to take a non-serving man?'

'If he is not on my staff,' said Heatherstone after a moment's thought, 'then I suppose you must do as you please.'

And with that he strode off, leaving Abel Corbould smiling his thin smile.

Eight

Trapped

OSWALD WANTED JACOB to stay overnight but he had never left the children alone before, so, in spite of his tiredness and the ache in his chest, he loaded the supplies on to the cart and headed for home.

He made the best speed he could but dawn was already breaking when he arrived at the cottage. There was no sign of life, not even a puff of smoke from the chimney.

'Look at that, Smoker. Haven't even got the sense to keep a fire going. How would they manage without us, eh?'

Painfully, the old forester climbed down from the

cart and, with the dog at his side, entered the cottage. In the gloom he could see Humphrey asleep in his usual place, on a straw mattress laid out in front of the fire. He prodded the boy with the toe of his boot.

'Up you get, young Humphrey, or you'll miss out on Maggie Partridge's venison stew.'

'What time is it?' groaned Humphrey.

'Time you was on your feet,' said Jacob. 'I want you to fetch some water.'

On the other side of the room Edward stirred and Alice appeared on the stairs.

'Jacob!' she said. 'We didn't expect you till later. You must have driven all night.'

'I thought it best to get back,' said Jacob.

Edward got up and began coaxing the fire to life. 'There,' he said as the first flames appeared, 'did I hear you say something about stew?'

'In a pot on the cart, along with our supplies,' said Jacob, as he lowered himself into a chair.

'Are you all right?' asked Alice.

The old man managed a smile. 'Just tired, that's all. But I found out plenty. For a start, Parliament has put a man in charge of the forest, an Intendant if you please. Man called Heatherstone, arrived yesterday with his daughter.'

'We saw them!' exclaimed Alice. 'On the Lymington road, they went by in a cart . . .'

'Did they see you?' asked Jacob.

'Yes, but they didn't take any notice,' said Edward, returning with a black cooking pot which he set on the fire.

'The girl did,' said Alice. 'She smiled at you.'

'She did not!' said Edward, blushing. 'Anyway, Jacob, what else did you find out? Anything about Aunt Judith?'

Jacob lowered his eyes. 'I'm afraid it looks like she died at Arnwood. At least, that's what Oswald Partridge says.'

'Which means the Roundheads killed her!' said Edward bitterly. 'They let her die in the fire!'

'It seems so. I'm sorry. She was a good woman.'

At that moment, the door flew open and Humphrey came crashing into the room. 'Roundheads!' he gasped, letting the bucket fall. 'Coming this way!'

'Did they see you?' asked Jacob.

'I don't think so.'

Jacob snatched the cooking pot off the fire and began kicking the burning embers aside.

'Right, up you go.' He patted the oak beam above the fireplace. 'You can stand on this if you're careful . . .'

With Jacob's help, the boys scrambled up into the darkness of the chimney, holding on to the hooks Jacob had fixed for hanging the venison. The brickwork was thick with soot and the boys soon stirred up a cloud which threatened to choke them.

'Keep still,' said Jacob, 'and remember, not a sound!'

He ducked out, to find that Edith had woken up and was standing on the stairs.

'Get her back to bed!' he whispered to Alice. 'She must pretend to have the fever. You stay with her.'

There was a loud hammering on the door. Alice ran up the stairs, collecting Edith on the way, and as she reached the top Jacob shouted to her, 'Your name!'

Alice looked at him blankly.

'What's your name?'

He meant the one he had asked her to make up.

'Er . . . Sarah!' she said, thinking quickly.

Jacob nodded, took a deep breath and opened the door.

Eight mounted troopers were drawn up outside the cottage, led by Abel Corbould. Smoker began barking at the horses, which shifted nervously.

'So, friends,' said Jacob, 'what can I do for you?'

'You can take hold of that dog,' said Hammond,

the sergeant who had lit the fire at the church, 'then you can show us some of your woodland hospitality.'

Jacob had no choice. The Levellers were already dismounting and all he could do was follow them indoors.

'Are you alone in the world, brother?' asked Abel Corbould. 'Or has the Lord blessed you with a family?'

'My granddaughters are upstairs,' said Jacob, 'on account of sickness in the family.'

At once Corbould gestured to one of his men to take a look.

'We need a guide, brother,' he said to Jacob, 'and I hear no one knows this forest better than you.'

Hammond meanwhile had found the cooking pot and was tasting the contents. 'You do yourselves proud out here in the wilderness. Venison stew, no less.'

'A man must live.' Jacob shrugged.

'And live very well, brother,' Hammond said and began to blow on the embers of the fire, which soon flickered back to life.

Up in the bedroom, Alice just had time to bundle Edith into bed before the trooper came in. Edith kept her eyes closed and pretended to shiver, although to tell the truth she was so frightened she didn't have to pretend very hard.

'What's the matter with her?' barked the trooper.

'Please, sir,' said Alice politely, 'it's the fever, sir.'

The man thought about this for a moment, then he took off one of his heavy leather gloves and made to put his hand on Edith's brow.

'Or . . . it could be the smallpox!' blurted Alice.

The trooper's hand froze in mid-air. Smallpox was a deadly disease and the trooper had no intention of risking his life over some forest brat.

'Leave her here,' he said to Alice. 'You come downstairs with me.'

Hammond piled wood on the fire and soon had a good blaze going, good enough to warm the stewpot and good enough to warm the boys' feet as they stood on the narrow beam a few inches above his head. The heat was scorching and the wood smoke made their eyes stream. They had to cover their mouths with their shirts or they would surely have started coughing and given the game away.

Jacob could see what was happening, but when he tried to get near the fire, Hammond stopped him.

'Why don't you get us some plates, old man?' said

the sergeant, and then he caught sight of Alice on the stairs.

'That's my Sarah,' said Jacob.

'Well then, Sarah, why don't you go with your grandfather and find that jug of ale he's got hidden away?'

There was nothing else for it. Even when the cooking pot came off the fire and Jacob tried to kick the logs away, Hammond would have none of it.

'Now, now, brother,' he said, handing Jacob the pot, 'surely you won't deny us a bit of warmth while we eat?'

And so while Jacob dished out the stew, Hammond threw on more wood so that, by the time the troopers were eating, the flames were licking hungrily up the chimney.

Nine

A Wild Goose Chase

ABEL CORBOULD MOPPED up the last of the stew with a piece of bread and leant back in his chair.

'We're searching for a priest,' he said, 'a man called Ratcliffe who once served the Beverleys of Arnwood.'

At the mention of the name Beverley, Alice's hand shook and she almost spilled the ale she was pouring.

'Maybe we should get started then,' said Jacob. 'We're wasting daylight . . .'.

'All in good time,' said Corbould. 'We'll also be looking for Beverley's children.'

'I thought they died at Arnwood,' said Jacob. 'Least ways, that's what I heard.'

'Did you now?' said Corbould. 'Well, I'm not so sure. One of them was a girl about your age, Sarah.'

Now Alice's hand really did shake, but help was at hand from an unexpected quarter.

Smoker had been left outside with the tethered horses and when one of them kicked out at him, he started barking. The horses began to panic and soon two or three of them tried to break loose.

The commotion could easily be heard in the cottage, even the boys up the chimney could hear it, and it soon brought Sergeant Hammond to his feet.

'Quickly, brothers,' he shouted, 'we're losing the horses!'

The troopers sprang up from the table and ran out into the yard. All except Abel Corbould, who remained seated as though nothing had happened.

'You seem very nervous, sister,' he said to Alice, who couldn't stop her hands from trembling.

'Reverend Corbould,' said Jacob, 'your men are waiting. Hadn't we better be on our way?'

Slowly Corbould got to his feet.

'You're right, brother. Duty calls, I'm afraid, Sarah,' and he gave a little bow and left the cottage.

As soon as he was gone, Jacob turned to Alice.

'Bar the door,' he whispered. 'Don't let anyone in, then see to the boys!'

Alice locked the door behind him, ran to the fire-place and began kicking the burning logs aside. Edith joined her and together they helped Edward, cough-ing and gasping, down from the chimney.

He was black from head to foot, the toes of his boots were smoking and his hands were burnt and bleeding where the iron hook had cut into them.

The girls ran back to the chimney and soon Humphrey, who if anything was even blacker than Edward, was slumped across the table beside his brother.

'That was close,' said Edward.

Humphrey nodded.

'But you know the worst of it?' Edward pointed at the empty cooking pot. 'Those Roundhead villains have eaten all our stew!'

Jacob Armitage led the Levellers through every stink-ing ditch and thorny thicket he could find. He was determined not to take them anywhere that the par-son might be hiding, and since they were all Londoners, that was easy for they hadn't a clue about the ways of the forest. Even so, when they passed Marl Pit Oak for the third time, Hammond reined in his horse.

'I'll swear we've been here before. He's leading us round in circles!'

'I'm leading you through the forest,' said Jacob. 'What you make of it's up to you.'

Corbould put a hand on Jacob's arm. His face had been scratched by thorns, he had lost his hat and he was just about managing to keep his temper.

'If Brother William is right,' he said, 'you're playing a dangerous game.'

'Any time you want me to go home,' said Jacob, 'you just say the word.' His chest was hurting badly and he was grey in the face from the effort of fighting the pain.

'What's the matter?' said Corbould, leaning close. 'Are you unwell?'

Jacob looked at him. 'Would it make any difference?'

Corbould smiled his thin smile. 'Lead on, brother,' he said.

Edward and Humphrey had scrubbed themselves clean and, since Jacob had traded all the venison and the Levellers had eaten all the stew, they decided to go hunting.

While they were away, Alice baked bread and

asked Edith to collect the eggs. The chickens were kept in a shelter at the side of the cottage. They made nests in the hay and you had to reach in and find the eggs.

She had only been gone for a minute when there was an ear-splitting scream. Alice seized the poker and ran to see what was wrong.

Edith was standing, white-faced, pointing down at the ground. 'Look!' she whispered. 'I touched it!'

Sticking out of the hay was a small, brown and rather grubby foot. Alice waved her poker at it.

'Out of there, you,' she said. 'I warn you, I have a poker and I'm not afraid to use it.'

After a moment the hay parted and the owner of the foot stood up. It was a boy, olive-skinned and brown-eyed, about the same age as Edith. There was a broken shell in his hand and egg-yolk running down his chin and dripping on to the assortment of rags that made up his clothes.

Just before sundown, Jacob led the Levellers out of the forest and back on to the Lymington road. They had spent hours in the saddle and had found precisely nothing, which was just what Jacob had intended.

'It's a straight road from here,' he said to Corbould. 'Better luck next time, eh?'

Corbould's smile had quite disappeared. 'And there will be a next time, Jacob Armitage,' he said grimly. 'You may depend upon it!'

With that he spurred his horse savagely and rode off, followed by his men.

When they had gone, Jacob realized just how ill he now felt. He had been on the road for a day and a night, and the pain was so bad that even the shallowest breath was agony. He was bone-weary and, if the pony had not known its way, he might not have made it back to the cottage at all. As it was, he turned into the forest, let the animal go at its own pace and trusted that sooner or later he would be delivered safely home.

Ten
Pablo

W HEN EDWARD AND Humphrey returned from hunting, the ragged boy was seated at the table tearing his way through a loaf of bread.

'I found him,' said Edith proudly, 'hiding with the chickens. He'd been eating eggs, not cooked or anything.'

'Where did he come from?' asked Edward. 'What's his name?'

'That's just it,' said Alice, 'we can't get a word out of him. He just sits there eating. That's his third loaf.'

Edward sat down opposite the boy and took what was left of the bread.

'Now listen here, you,' he said in his best 'High Keeper of the King's Forest' voice. 'If you're going to sit there scoffing our bread, you'd jolly well better answer some questions. We want to know who you are and where you come from.'

But the boy said nothing. In fact, his eyes never left the loaf.

'Do you think he's . . . you know, a half-wit?' asked Humphrey.

The others looked at the boy, who seemed far from stupid and was pretty obviously planning how to get his bread back.

'He's got a very good colour,' said Alice. 'Do you think he might be foreign?'

'What, like a Frenchie?' asked Edward.

'Yes, or a Spaniard . . .'

For the first time the boy took his eyes off the bread. '*España, si!*' he said clearly.

'Now we're getting somewhere,' said Edward. 'Well done, Alice,' and he waved the bread under the ragged boy's nose. 'Now see here, young Spaniard, we're going to ask you some questions and every time we get an answer, you get a piece of bread. *Comprendez?*'

The boy looked at Edward, then he looked at the bread. '*Si,*' he said.

'Excellent,' said Edward with a smile. 'Edith, fetch another loaf!'

An hour later, darkness had fallen, Alice had put a lamp in the window to light Jacob home and the ragged boy had eaten all the bread in the cottage.

However, they had found out some interesting things about him. His name was Pablo, he came from Spain and he had been with the army until someone sold him to a band of outlaws, from whom he had run away.

Smoker had been lying quietly by the hearth, but as the boy finished his story he got up and began whining at the door.

'Oh, good,' said Alice, 'Jacob's back!' and she went to let him in.

The others looked Pablo up and down.

'Do you think he's telling the truth?' asked Humphrey. 'He looks pretty weedy to be an outlaw . . .'

Just then a strange voice made them all turn to the door.

'Good evening, one and all! Christopher Taggart at your service, and this is my associate, Mr Fancy.'

The two men who stood before them were both above thirty years old and were both wearing clothes that might once have been of good quality. However, that was long ago and a more villainous-looking pair it would have been hard to imagine, particularly the one calling himself Taggart. He had a sharp, beak-like nose, thin bloodless lips and he carried a battered hat with a plume that he twirled constantly as he spoke.

'Ah, there he is!' Taggart pointed at Pablo. 'I hope he hasn't been making a nuisance of himself.'

Pablo tried to hide under the table, but in one quick movement Taggart had him by the scruff of the neck and held him, choking, with his feet just off the ground.

'Upsadaisy! Let's leave these good people in peace, shall we? Thank you for looking after him. Come along, Mr Fancy –'

'Just a moment,' said Edward, stepping forward. 'I think you should leave him alone.'

'Do you now?'

Taggart looked Edward up and down. The boy was taller, by two or three inches, but Taggart was stronger, much stronger.

'Yes, it's quite obvious he doesn't want to go with you,' said Edward.

Taggart's lip curled. 'Yes, well, we can't all have what we want in life, can we? I'm his dear papa and he must do as he's told.'

'You're not his papa!' exclaimed Edith. 'You're an outlaw!'

'An outlaw I may be,' said Taggart, 'but I paid good money for this one to the King's own Baggage Master. He's mine fair and square, same as if I was his father.'

'Let him go,' said Edward, blocking the man's way.

'Oh, now just a minute . . .'

Taggart passed Pablo to his crony and stepped in close until Edward could smell onions and cheap brandy on his breath.

'I've been nice to you, I've been polite. I haven't come in here pushing you about and trying to make off with your property. So why don't you just *leave me alone*!' he shouted right into Edward's face.

Edward couldn't help himself, he flinched and looked away.

'See that, Mr Fancy?' Taggart clearly thought he'd won. 'Mr Fancy?'

Mr Fancy didn't answer, not because he didn't want to, but because Jacob Armitage had crept through the open door and bent the poker round his neck and this was interfering with his breathing. In fact, all Fancy could do was choke until Jacob let him go and he fell, gasping, to the floor. Then, without any apparent effort, Jacob straightened the poker and handed it to Alice.

'Someone must have left this outside,' he said quietly. 'Put it back in the hearth for me, would you?' Jacob did not take his eyes off Taggart. 'Now, my friend,' he said, 'I suggest you get on your way, while you can still walk.'

Taggart twirled the plume on his hat.

'Yes. What a good idea! I'll just give poor Mr Fancy a hand, if I may . . .'

He bent down as if to help his friend, then slashed his hat across Jacob's face and threw a punch that would certainly have sent the forester sprawling if it had ever landed. But Jacob caught the man's fist in his own huge hand and squeezed until the children heard something crack and Taggart let out a yell of pain.

By this time Mr Fancy was attempting to get to his feet. Jacob took both outlaws by the collar, banged their heads together with a crunch that could have been heard in Lymington and kicked them out into the yard, where they lay, gasping, in the dirt.

He stood over them and his voice was harsh and rasping. 'I don't want to see either of you ever again, not here, not anywhere! Do you understand?'

'Oh yes, we understand,' said Taggart, rubbing his head. 'You have a way of putting things, a talent you might say. Come along, Mr Fancy. We're not wanted here. Shift yourself . . .'

And he pulled Fancy to his feet and both of them limped off into the darkness.

Edith clapped her hands in delight. 'Jacob saved your life!' she said to Pablo. 'You can stay with us now. Can't he, Jacob?'

But all the strength had left Jacob and he had slumped down in the yard. This last great effort had been too much for him and he clutched helplessly at his chest.

'Jacob, Jacob!' cried Alice. 'What's the matter?'

'Help me get him inside,' said Edward.

But Jacob would not let them move him. Instead he beckoned Edward to come closer.

'Listen to me! You must seek out . . .' His voice dropped almost to a whisper but the next word sounded like 'tunnel'.

'Seek out a tunnel, yes,' said Edward. 'Where?'

'Turbary Bower,' gasped Jacob. 'The Levellers must not find it.' He tried to say more but the words would not come.

'Please, Jacob,' said Edith. 'Don't be ill.'

The old forester reached out his hand and gently

touched her face. 'I'm sorry, little 'un,' he managed to say, and then he smiled at her and Jacob Armitage closed his eyes for the last time.

Eleven

Alone

THE CHILDREN BURIED Jacob at the foot of a great chestnut tree on the edge of the clearing. Edward read a passage from the Bible, Edith laid wild flowers on the turned earth and Humphrey made a cross out of wood to mark the grave.

'Goodbye, Jacob,' said Alice. 'I know you'll still watch over us.'

'And I promise to make myself useful and help Alice,' said Edith.

'Goodbye, old Jacob,' said Pablo. 'I never know you but you save my life. *Gracias.*'

'He saved all our lives,' said Edward, 'and we will always remember him.'

*

Later the children cooked a meal and Edward said grace just as Jacob had always done, but no one felt very much like eating.

Alice kept thinking about what Jacob had said, about the tunnel and the place called Turbary Bower, but Edward had never heard of it.

'We'd need to ask the other foresters,' he said. 'They might know.'

'Then, Edward, you should go and see Oswald Partridge,' said Alice. 'In any case, you ought to tell him about Jacob.'

Edward didn't want to leave them, but at the same time he could see it made good sense. So he took Jacob's musket and went out to saddle the pony.

Humphrey came to help and looked nervously at the musket. 'Don't go in carrying that,' he said. 'There are bound to be Roundheads near Keeper's Cottage.'

Edward promised to hide it at the Marl Pit Oak and then collect it on the way home.

'And what about that,' said Humphrey, pointing to Edward's gold crucifix.

'I'll keep it hidden,' he said, tucking the chain inside his shirt.

Humphrey laughed. 'You might just as well carry a sign saying, "Edward Beverley, please arrest me"!'

'I said I'll keep it hidden! Now come on and help me find Smoker. I want to take him with me.'

'There he is,' said Humphrey, pointing towards Jacob's grave.

Sure enough, the dog was lying there as if he expected his master to return at any moment.

'Come on, old chap,' said Edward. 'Let's go hunting!'

'Rabbits, Smoker!' said Humphrey.

But it took a great deal of coaxing to persuade the dog to leave, and at the edge of the clearing he turned back and barked three times, as if he was saying goodbye to old Jacob, before following Edward and the pony.

The Marl Pit Oak stood at a crossroads about two or three miles from Keeper's Cottage and by the time Edward got there it was already past midday. Smoker watched him climb into the lower branches, where he hid the musket, together with his powder and shot, taking special care to wrap the powder horn in a piece of cloth to stop it getting damp.

As he jumped down from the tree, he felt his father's crucifix jump on the chain at his throat. Was Humphrey right, he wondered, should he leave it?

No, he couldn't be parted from it. He tucked it back into his shirt and rode on.

It was mid-afternoon when he arrived and Oswald Partridge was overjoyed to see him. Much as he was saddened to hear about Jacob, he was delighted to know that all four Beverley children were alive and well.

Edward asked about the Levellers and Oswald told him that things were better since the new Intendant, Mr Heatherstone, had been in charge. Edward said he had seen Heatherstone the day he arrived.

'Then you'll have seen the daughter, Miss Patience,' said Oswald. 'She's a pretty one, eh?'

Edward could feel himself blushing. So that was her name, Patience . . .

'Oh, is she?' he said carelessly. 'I can't say I noticed.'

'Oh, didn't you?' Oswald smiled, but then he looked at Edward and his face became serious. 'It must be very hard for you, hiding out in the forest with the likes of Corbould strutting about.'

'It is,' said Edward. 'I'd do anything to strike a blow for His Majesty!'

'Would you now?' Oswald got up from the fireside. 'Well, I've got something here might help you do just that . . .'

He reached into the space above one of the low ceiling beams and handed Edward a long object wrapped in sacking. When the cloth was unwound, there inside, oiled and gleaming, lay a sword.

'My father's?' asked Edward.

'The very same. Placed in these hands as he lay dying on the field at Naseby.'

The blade had been well cared for and Edward's eyes shone as he held it aloft. Oswald watched him.

'You know they say the King has fled and is likely heading for these parts?'

'Is that true?'

Oswald shrugged. 'It's what they say,' he said simply.

'Then we must be ready!' cried Edward. 'Oswald, just before Jacob died he mentioned a tunnel at a place called Turbary Bower. He said the Round-heads must never find it. Does that mean anything to you?'

Oswald thought for a moment. 'I know Turbary Bower, but I know of no tunnel.'

'I've a feeling it's important,' said Edward, 'not just for me but for the King. Will you show me the way?'

'Gladly,' said Oswald, 'but it's a fair stretch. If you're going there, you'd better stay the night.'

And so it was settled. Edward would spend the night in the stable loft and set out at first light for Turbary Bower. He returned the sword to its sacking and handed it back to Oswald.

'Keep it for me,' he said. 'I'll know where to find it when the right time comes.'

Twelve

Smoke and Fire

T HE STABLE OVERLOOKED the courtyard
behind the old parsonage, the house that had been
taken over by the Roundheads. Edward made himself a bed of clean straw and then, taking care not
to be seen, he settled down at the loft window and
watched the comings and goings in the yard below.

He saw Abel Corbould conducting evening
prayers with a group of his Levellers. They sang their
psalms and Corbould preached a fiery sermon and
then, when they had gone inside, Edward heard the
sound of a horse's hooves as Patience Heatherstone
rode into the yard.

She was every bit as beautiful as Edward

remembered her. Her green eyes were bright from the excitement of the ride and, although she was still dressed in Puritan black, her red hair had come loose and fell gleaming about her shoulders.

She exchanged a few words with the groom and then she disappeared inside the house. A minute or two later, lamplight shone at an upper window and there she was, this time accompanied by the woman Edward had seen that first day on the cart. They spoke for a while and then the woman drew the curtains and Edward could see no more.

It was almost dark and Edward had a long day ahead of him, so he settled down on the straw and, with Smoker curled up at his feet, did his best to go to sleep. He must have dozed, because the next thing he knew, moonlight was streaming through the loft window and Smoker was looking out and whining softly.

'Smoker, lie down!' said Edward, but the dog wouldn't settle and began to bark.

Afraid he would waken the whole household, Edward got up to close the shutters and then saw, across the courtyard, a thick plume of smoke billowing from Patience Heatherstone's window.

Seizing his jacket, he scrambled down the stairway and out into the yard. No lights were showing, the whole house was asleep, but as Edward looked around he saw that the servants had left some iron cooking pots near the water pump. Grabbing the two largest, he began to bang them together as loudly as he could.

'Fire!' he shouted. 'Come on, stir yourselves! There's a fire!'

At last lights appeared, and one by one the servants stumbled sleepily into the yard.

'That's Miss Patience's chamber!' said one, catching sight of the smoke.

A small crowd of servants had gathered, along with one or two of Corbould's men, but they were all milling about helplessly. Edward took control.

'Fetch anything you can find to carry water,' he shouted, 'then form a line to the pump.'

By the time he had shown them what he wanted, Oswald Partridge had arrived with a ladder, which was quickly set against the wall of the house. Then, wrapping his jacket about his right arm, Edward climbed up and looked in at the window.

The curtains were drawn and the windows securely fastened, so, using the protection of his jacket, Edward punched through the glass. When the fresh air reached the fire, a huge gout of flame spurted from the window, burning Edward's arm clear through the jacket and almost forcing him off the ladder. Somehow he held on, and the servants began to pass up buckets, pots, pans, all of which Edward emptied through the window as best he could.

'Can you see inside?' shouted Oswald.

'No, I'll have to go in,' said Edward, and, taking the jacket off his arm, he began to soak it in water from one of the pots. Then, using it to protect his face, he climbed over the window-ledge and into the room.

The curtains of the four-poster bed were well alight but the bed itself was not touched and lying on it he could just make out the shape of Patience Heatherstone.

Edward tore at the hangings, which were evidently where the fire had started. As for the girl, her face was deathly pale, but at least she was still breathing. Edward managed to raise her into a sitting position and from there lift her across his shoulders. Then, as the flames began licking at the bed, he hauled himself to his feet and groped his way back towards the window.

Down in the courtyard the servants had fallen silent

but all eyes were on the bedroom window. A great cheer went up when Edward appeared at the top of the ladder with Patience in his arms. She was passed gently down and soon Oswald announced that she was breathing normally and would very likely recover.

Edward's jacket was burnt and his shirt was in smoke-stained tatters, but apart from his arm he too was safe and sound.

'If it wasn't for you, she'd be dead for sure,' said one of Corbould's Levellers, clapping him on the back. 'What's your name, lad?'

'Er . . . Armitage,' said Edward quickly, 'Edward Armitage.'

'Three cheers for Master Armitage!' shouted the trooper.

'No, no!' said Edward. 'I was just happy to help . . .'

He started to back away through the crowd, but then he felt a hand on his shoulder.

'Not leaving us already, are you, Master Armitage?' said Abel Corbould. 'Or should I say Master Beverley?'

He reached forward and took Edward's crucifix, clearly visible through the torn shirt, and wrenched it from his neck.

Edward looked for a way out, but other Levellers were already pushing forward through the crowd. 'Seize him!' shouted Abel Corbould.

Thirteen
Under Arrest

T<small>HE INTENDANT LET</small> the chain of the crucifix run slowly through his fingers.

'Tell me, Edward Beverley,' he said, 'of what crime are you accused?'

'Sir,' said Edward, 'I know of none.'

They were standing in Heatherstone's study, Edward, two Leveller guards and Corbould, and Corbould couldn't believe his ears.

'He is Edward Beverley!' said the preacher. 'Son of Squire Beverley, Master of Arnwood!'

Heatherstone's face was pale and drawn but his voice was determined. 'Come now, Reverend Corbould, if a man's name is a crime we must lock up half of England. I want to know of what he is accused.'

Edward hardly dared breathe. It sounded as though Heatherstone was on his side, and what is more Corbould thought so too. He strode over to the Intendant and lowered his voice to a whisper.

'Don't play games! You know the King is on the run. Who will he turn to if not the son of his dead henchman?'

'This boy saved my daughter's life. You expect me to imprison him for what the King might do?'

'Most certainly,' said Corbould, 'and his brother and sisters along with him.'

'That cannot be right,' said Heatherstone. 'We are not sent to make war on children.'

'Listen to me,' said Corbould, 'when you go hunting rats and you find a nest of young ones, do you leave them to grow mischievous? No, you squeeze them while you can.' He produced a sheet of parchment and thrust it in front of Heatherstone. 'See, the warrant is drawn up. Sign it and I will take them all to London. The matter will be off your hands.'

'But not off my conscience,' replied Heatherstone. 'If London wants them, then London must sign. You'll get no warrant from me!'

Corbould was suddenly very calm and quiet. He

folded the parchment, slipped it back into his tunic and went over to Edward.

'Give my regards to Jacob Armitage,' he said.

'He's dead,' said Edward. 'Jacob is dead.'

'Then he will make his peace with God,' said the preacher. 'You, however, will make your peace with me. This is not finished!' He nodded to the two troopers and silently they followed him out of the room.

Half an hour later Edward was seated by the fire in Keeper's Cottage and Patience Heatherstone was dressing his burnt arm.

'Let me know if I hurt you,' she said as she put ointment on a cloth and began to smear it gently on to the wound.

'It's all right,' he said. 'I mean it hurts, obviously, but it's all right . . .'

Patience worked on in silence for a while and then she said, 'Well, well, well, Edward Beverley. I had no idea I was mixing with nobility. It was you I saw that day on the road, wasn't it? Were you with your sister?'

'Alice. Yes.'

'Are there any more of you?'

'Another sister and a brother.'

'I'd like to meet them. Are they all like you?'

69

'I hope not, for their sake,' said Edward, and for the first time Patience looked up at him.

'Oh, I don't know,' she said, 'you're not so bad.'

Edward smiled, then quickly looked away. 'How are you,' he said, 'after last night?'

'My head hurts, that's all. And I wouldn't be here at all if it wasn't for you, so please don't say it was nothing.'

Actually Edward wasn't going to say anything of the kind. He thought it was pretty impressive.

'And I never even said "thank you",' said Patience, 'so, thank you, Edward,' and she leant forward and kissed him on the cheek.

Edward was taken by surprise but this was definitely not the time to be shy.

'It was a pleasure, Patience,' he said, and kissed her gently on the lips, just as the housekeeper, Phoebe, walked into the room.

Edward and Patience sprang apart as if they'd been scalded.

'Phoebe!' said Patience. 'Edward burnt his arm, I was just . . .'

'Were you "just"?' said Phoebe sternly. 'Mistress Partridge said I might find you here. Well, your father wants to see you . . . Both of you.'

*

From Mr Heatherstone's study it was possible to look directly into the courtyard, where Abel Corbould was conducting another prayer meeting for his Levellers. The chanting of their psalms was drifting into the room as Edward and Patience entered.

'If Corbould sends to London to get his warrant signed, you've got two, perhaps three days,' said Mr Heatherstone.

'But, Father,' said Patience, 'if Edward has done nothing wrong, why must he be hounded like this?'

Heatherstone sighed. 'The King has escaped and Corbould thinks he may come to the forest. If he does, then perhaps Edward Beverley might try to help him.'

'Perhaps I might,' said Edward, 'but I know nothing of this.'

'There you are,' said Patience. 'Surely you can protect him?'

Heatherstone shook his head. 'Not unless he swears to uphold the laws of Parliament, which I assume he will not . . .'

They both looked at Edward, but he remained silent. As High Keeper of the King's Forest, he could answer only to His Majesty.

'I owe you my daughter's life,' said Heatherstone, 'and now I have paid my debt. You are free to go, but you must not return here or speak with Patience again.'

'And what about Patience?' Her green eyes flashed as she spoke. 'May we not hear what she has to say?'

'No, we may not!' Heatherstone's voice was final. 'She will do her duty to her father as he will to her!' He took Edward's crucifix from the table and gave it to him. 'You are a marked man, Edward Beverley. I advise you to look to your family and leave me to look to mine.'

Fourteen

Turbary Bower

O SWALD PARTRIDGE WALKED with Edward as far as the Marl Pit Oak, where his musket was hidden.

'Is your powder dry?' asked Oswald.

'It should be,' said Edward as he handed it down. 'I wrapped it double . . .'

'Well, don't you rely on it till you've tried it,' said Oswald. 'Now then, Turbary Bower . . . four, maybe five miles past the Marl Pit, you'll see an old charcoal burner's hut, been empty for years.'

'But no tunnel?' said Edward.

Oswald shrugged. 'Not as I know of, but then I've never had a reason to go looking.'

Edward said farewell to Oswald and, with Smoker trotting behind him, rode out of the forest and up on to the open heath, where the wild ponies grazed and where herds of deer bounded away as he approached.

As he rode along, he couldn't help thinking about Patience Heatherstone. Not so very long ago he'd believed that the only good Roundhead was a dead Roundhead, but now the thought that he might never see her again made him hate the civil war and everything that had come between them.

These thoughts were still with him when the forest closed in once more and he found himself following a track between tall and gloomy beech trees. Then, at a point where the track divided, he heard a pistol shot away to his left. He dismounted, tethered the pony and, after calling Smoker to heel, crept forward towards the sound of the gunfire.

Soon the trees thinned and Edward found himself looking down into a clearing. There was a small thatched cottage and judging by the moss-covered stacks of logs lying about, this was the old charcoal burner's hut, but, far from being empty, it was occupied by someone who was determined to remain inside. A pair of pistols appeared at the window and the owner fired them blindly towards the log piles.

At first Edward could not see what he was firing at and was just about to move in for a closer look, when a familiar voice rang out.

'Now just a minute! I've been nice to you, I've been polite. I haven't come in here pushing you about and trying to make off with your property . . .'

Taggart! It was Taggart the outlaw who had fought with Jacob at the cottage. Even Smoker recognized that sneering voice and he growled softly. But what was a scoundrel like Taggart doing out here and, more to the point, was there anyone else with him?

The second question was soon answered when Fancy and another man appeared from behind one of the log pile and made a rush for the hut while the owner of the pistols was reloading. Fancy took cover beneath the window, but his companion was not quite quick enough. He was still out in the open when the pistol barrels reappeared. There was a deafening roar, a cloud of smoke and the man took both shots full in the chest. He let out a cry and pitched forward on to the ground, as dead as mutton.

Now it was Taggart's chance to move in. He popped up from behind his log pile and, in a crouching run, crossed the clearing and threw himself down beside Fancy. There he produced a pistol of his own and, from what Edward could judge, began persuading Fancy to break down the door while he covered him from the window.

At first Fancy didn't seem keen, but in the end he must have agreed because Edward saw him crawl into position. Then, on a signal from Taggart, he let out a fearsome yell, kicked the cabin door open and hurled himself inside.

Immediately there was a shot and a scream, and only then did Taggart stand up and fire through the window.

'The villain!' thought Edward. Far from covering his friend, he had actually used Fancy to draw the other man's fire. Taggart was now peering through the window and, having decided that the coast was clear, he strolled calmly to the door and disappeared inside the hut.

Edward quickly loaded his musket and ran across the clearing, stopping under the window as Taggart had done, before cautiously raising his head and looking into the room.

There were two bodies on the floor. The occupant of the hut had clearly been killed by Taggart, but not before he had shot Fancy. Taggart was now searching the room with his back to the window and both he and Edward heard the sound of crying at the same time.

At first Edward could not work out where it was coming from, but then Taggart threw aside an upturned table and there, hiding underneath, was a young girl, about nine or ten years old, and she was struggling frantically to load a pistol.

With a sudden shock, Edward realized that he knew her. It was Clara Ratcliffe, the parson's daughter . . . which meant that the other dead man must be her father. As Taggart took hold of the girl and pulled her roughly to her feet, Edward brought the musket to his shoulder and stepped into the room.

'Let her go!'

Taggart spun around, holding Clara in front of him, and at the same time snatching the pistol she had been loading. But when he recognized Edward, he gave a sigh of relief.

'Oh, it's you!' he said. 'For a minute I thought it might be somebody dangerous.'

'Let her go,' Edward repeated, cocking the musket and making it ready to fire.

Taggart wasn't impressed. 'You've tried ordering me about, remember? It doesn't work.'

'I'm not afraid to use this, you know,' said Edward.

'Oh, yes you are,' smirked Taggart, cocking his own pistol.

Edward knew it was now or never. He took a deep breath and fired, but the musket clicked harmlessly. Nothing happened.

'Oh, what a shame!' said Taggart. 'Damp powder? Now, it's my turn . . .'

Slowly and deliberately, he levelled the pistol at Edward, but as his finger tightened on the trigger there was a terrifying snarl and a grey shape appeared at the doorway and leapt across the room. The outlaw just had time to put up his right arm, and the next second Smoker's jaws clamped on.

For a moment they hung there, man and dog equally balanced, then Taggart recovered. Throwing Clara aside, he switched the pistol to his left hand and, at point-blank range, fired at the dog, who let out one agonized yelp and fell like a stone.

'Smoker!' cried Edward, and swung the musket as hard as he could at Taggart.

The heavy wooden stock caught the outlaw square on the jaw and he was unconscious before he hit the floor. But one look told Edward that it was too late for Smoker. The musket ball had taken him just behind the shoulder and he had died instantly.

Although Edward felt hot tears pricking at his eyes, he was comforted by the thought that at least the faithful hound had not suffered.

Fifteen

Night Visitors

By the time Edward had got Clara back to the cottage, darkness had fallen, but Alice had left a lamp burning in the window to light him home. As soon as they arrived, she came running out with Edith, who helped carry Clara up to Jacob's room. There they unwrapped her heavy cloak and put her to bed, but she did not open her eyes and her face was hot and flushed.

'What's the matter with her?' asked Edith. 'Is she hurt?'

'I don't think so,' replied Edward. 'It must be some kind of fever. She was hiding with her father at

Turbary Bower. Poor Parson Ratcliffe was shot by Taggart and his men.'

Alice brought some milk and tried to get Clara to drink a little, but as soon as the girl opened her eyes she wanted desperately to talk to Edward.

'You must go back,' she gasped, 'back to Turbary Bower! There's a chest hidden in the roof, the Roundheads must never find it . . . It's to do with you, and the King. And there's a letter, look for a letter! I was writing it when the robbers came . . .'

She wanted to say more but was overcome by a fit of coughing. Alice laid her back gently on the pillows. Edward, however, had heard enough. He left the room and went downstairs to find Humphrey and Pablo.

'Come on, you two,' he said. 'Help me get the pony harnessed. We're going back to Turbary Bower.'

Humphrey picked up the musket from the table. 'Then hadn't we better take this?' he asked.

'No point,' said Edward, steering them towards the door, 'the powder's damp. But if we're quick we shan't need it. We'll be in and out before anyone knows we're there.'

*

It was after midnight when the boys arrived at Turbary Bower. The hut was in darkness and Edward wondered if perhaps Taggart was still inside. Although he'd hit the man hard, he didn't believe he'd killed him and if he was still around there could be trouble.

Inside, the darkness was total. Working only by touch, Edward struck tinder and lit the stub of candle. The two younger boys let out a gasp when the light flickered on the lifeless bodies of Fancy and Parson Ratcliffe. Edward, on the other hand, was relieved that there was no sign of Taggart. The villain had evidently recovered and gone on his way.

'Is he dead?' asked Humphrey, looking at Fancy.

'Oh, *si*,' replied Pablo, 'like in the war. He is shot through his eye. Look . . .'

Humphrey didn't really want to look, and fortunately for him Edward was soon calling for their help. He had found some loose boards in the ceiling of the hut and, while Humphrey held the candle, he reached into the space above and dragged out a wooden chest which Edward immediately recognized. It had belonged to his father. The box was strongly made, bound with iron bands and securely locked.

'Maybe we find something to break it open,' suggested Pablo, looking about him.

'No,' said Edward not wanting to linger, 'let's get

it back to the cottage. Now, Clara said to look for a letter . . . Can anyone see a letter? Humphrey, can you see a letter?'

But Humphrey wasn't listening. He was staring in horror at Smoker, who was lying where he had fallen after his brave attack on Taggart. With all that had happened, Edward had not even thought to mention him.

'I'm sorry,' he said. 'I should have told you.'

'You never said,' said Humphrey quietly.

'I know, I'm sorry, he saved my life . . . But there's nothing to be done and I'm afraid we must go.'

'We're not leaving him here!' said Humphrey fiercely. 'We're not!'

Edward could see his brother was determined and, what is more, he knew that he was right. 'Yes, of course we must take him,' he said. 'You two carry the chest and I'll bring Smoker.'

It was a sad little procession that left the hut, Humphrey and Pablo struggling with the strongbox and Edward carrying poor Smoker. In silence they climbed aboard the cart, in silence they drove away, and it was only when they were half-way home that Edward remembered, they had still not found Clara's letter.

*

While the boys were away, Alice and Edith took turns to sit with Clara and in the early hours of the morning there was a knock on the cottage door. Alice seized the musket and pointed it at the door, then signalled Edith to open it. There, on the step, was a mysterious figure, cloaked and hooded.

'Step forward,' said Alice, 'into the light, where I can see you.'

'Where's Edward?' asked the figure in a decidedly female voice.

'None of your business,' said Alice. 'Step forward and tell me who you are.'

Their visitor came into the room and threw back her hood to reveal a cascade of red hair. 'I'm Patience Heatherstone,' she said. 'Now, where's Edward? You're in great danger. You must believe me! I'm a good friend of your brother's.'

Alice gestured with the barrel of the gun for her to sit. 'My brother says the only good Roundhead is a dead Roundhead,' she said, and she cocked the musket and kept it pointing straight at Patience Heatherstone.

Sixteen

The Treasure Chest

WHEN EDWARD AND the boys arrived back at the cottage, Edith and Alice were both keeping guard on Patience, who hadn't been allowed to move an inch.

Humphrey couldn't believe his eyes. 'What's she doing here?' he asked. 'Isn't she a . . . a . . .'

'A Roundhead,' said Edith, 'yes, we know.'

'Apparently she's a friend of Edward's,' said Alice.

Edward put the chest down on the table and for the first time Alice lowered the musket slightly.

At once Patience sprang to her feet. 'Edward, they won't listen to me. Cromwell is in Winchester and Corbould has sent there to have the warrant signed.

I overheard him talking to Sergeant Hammond. When he gets back they'll be here to arrest you . . . all of you!'

'Thank you for the warning,' said Edward, 'I appreciate it, but first we have to open this. Alice, can you go and see if Clara has the key?'

Alice didn't reply. Instead she raised the musket until it was pointing once more at Patience.

'Come on, Alice,' said Edward. 'This is important. Don't you recognize this chest? It's father's.'

'Of course I recognize it,' said Alice, 'and you're surely not going to open it in front of her?'

'Why not?' said Edward. 'It's all right . . .'

Patience folded her arms. 'Your sister thinks I'm some sort of enemy spy. She's spent half the night pointing a musket at me.'

Edward couldn't help smiling. 'Oh, has she? Well, fortunately you were quite safe. It's the powder, you see, it's –'

He didn't get any further. There was a loud bang, the room filled with smoke and the lid of the chest flew open. Alice had shot off the lock.

'What were you saying about the powder?' asked Patience calmly.

'It's dried out,' said Humphrey.

Alice handed the musket to Edward. 'Your box is

open. You must do as you please. I shall be with Clara,' she said, and went upstairs.

Inside the chest were lots of things the children recognized from when they were young. There was Edith's silver christening plate, a gold locket of their mother's and many other things, including a leather pouch full of gold crowns.

Edward left Edith and Humphrey sorting through the box and went outside to say goodbye to Patience. Dawn was breaking and she was anxious to get home before she was missed.

When Edward returned, Humphrey had found a collection of papers hidden among the treasure. Some looked like letters written in code, but there was also a list of names. Edward took the list upstairs, along with the gold locket.

Clara was still sleeping. Her fever had not yet broken and Alice was bathing her face with water. As soon as she saw the locket, Alice knew what it was.

'Mother's.'

Edward nodded. 'She always wanted you to have it. And look at this.' He handed over the list. 'Every man in the forest who could be relied upon to help the King, along with their code names.'

'Parson Ratcliffe's code name was Tonnelier.'

Alice was thinking back to that terrible night outside the cottage and Jacob's last words. 'We thought Jacob was saying "tunnel" but he was really saying "Tonnelier". He knew Parson Ratcliffe was hiding at Turbary Bower!'

Edward was pacing the room. 'We must find the others, tell them all that Parson Ratcliffe is dead.'

'What about the letter?' asked Alice. 'Clara said there was a letter . . . Suppose it was important?'

Edward shrugged. 'What does it matter? The important thing is that Tonnelier is dead and they've all got to be warned.'

Seventeen
Prisoners

ALICE WAS RIGHT. The letter was important. As soon as Christopher Taggart saw it, he knew it was important, even though he couldn't read. It had an important-looking wax seal on it and Taggart's first thought was that someone might pay good money for such a letter. And that is what brought him to the door of Abel Corbould.

Corbould was having a very good day. His morning prayers had been disturbed . . . no, they had been *answered* by the arrival of Sergeant Hammond, who had made excellent time from Winchester and carried with him two warrants signed in Oliver Cromwell's own hand, one for the arrest of Edward

Beverley and the other for the arrest of Heatherstone, both on charges of treason.

Now Corbould was sitting in the very chair where yesterday the traitor Heatherstone had let Beverley go scot-free. How the world turned! And now here was this vagabond offering him the King's head on a plate, for Corbould was certain that the letter concerned the King. He spread it out on the table in front of him and read it for the tenth time.

'To my loyal Tonnelier,' it began, 'make all ready to receive our friend. He will come to you as we have arranged. Pray look for him when the moon is full . . .'

'Tonnelier', that was obviously Ratcliffe, the priest, and who was 'our friend' if not the Man of Blood himself? Charles Stuart, the King of England! And tonight was the full moon . . . Corbould could not believe his good fortune, but he gave nothing away as he looked at the rogue who had brought him the letter.

'You say the man Ratcliffe is dead?'

Taggart held his hat over his heart. 'Yes, your reverence, very sad. Shot by outlaws. We disturbed them, see, me and my two associates. Samaritans both, who fought the good fight and have gone to their eternal reward. And speaking of rewards . . .'

Corbould's pale eyes stared unblinkingly. 'What else did you take from the priest? There must have been something else.'

'Nothing, I swear.'

It was just a flicker of the eyes, but Corbould signalled to one of his Levellers and the trooper brought his armoured fist crashing down on the outlaw's neck, sending him sprawling across the table. As quick as a striking snake, Corbould pinned him there and spoke quietly into his ear.

'What else did you take?'

'Nothing, reverend!' gasped Taggart. 'Would I lie to a man of the cloth?' Corbould tightened his grip and Taggart's voice became a desperate squeak. 'Anyway, we weren't the only ones! What about the outlaws? There was a tall lad, I recognized him, I know where he lives. Friend of that old forester . . .'

'Beverley!' Slowly Corbould released the outlaw and smiled his thin smile. 'Lock this villain in the cellar,' he said to his men, 'then meet me at the stables. We have an appointment with Edward Beverley!'

Clara Ratcliffe was still too ill to be moved. The girls stayed with her and also hid the treasure chest in the chimney. They had just managed to brush themselves clean of soot when they heard Clara calling. She was awake and shouting for Edward.

'It's all right,' said Alice. 'He's gone with the boys to tell the people on the list about your father . . .'

'But what about the letter?' asked Clara.

Alice shook her head. 'He didn't find it. But don't worry, he'll warn everyone . . .'

'You don't understand,' said Clara. 'Yesterday morning my father got a message. The King is coming to the forest. The people on that list must help him get away to France. I was writing to them when the robbers came.'

'And how long before the King arrives?' asked Alice.

'We must look for him at the full moon.'

'But that's tonight!' gasped Alice.

'Exactly,' said Clara, sinking back in despair.

Edith was busy fastening back the shutters when she saw movement beyond the trees at the edge of the clearing. With a shock she realized it was horsemen approaching.

'Alice!' she cried. 'Troopers coming!'

Alice joined her at the window, but it was already too late. Corbould and his men were galloping across the clearing, and a few seconds later the girls heard the sound of splintering wood, followed by the heavy tread of boots on the stairs.

Corbould was furious not to find Edward in the cottage and was not about to show any mercy to the girls. In spite of Clara's fever, he ordered that they be thrown across the troopers' saddles and taken back to the Intendant's house.

The ride through the forest was long and hard. Branches and briars tore at their faces and, when at last the journey came to an end, Clara was once more unconscious. As the Levellers rode into the courtyard Patience Heatherstone appeared and tried to help, but the troopers held her back.

She turned on Corbould, eyes flashing. 'This child is sick!' she cried. 'Do you allow your men to ill-treat sick children?'

'They are enemies of the state,' said Corbould. 'Now stand clear!'

Clara and Edith were both taken indoors, but since Alice was able to dismount on her own, Patience managed to get close to her.

'They've arrested my father!' she whispered.

Alice reached out to her and, as their fingers touched, she pressed her mother's locket into

Patience's hand. 'Do you know King's Mill?' she asked softly.

'I can find it,' said Patience.

'Edward and the boys will be there. Give that to him and let him know we've been brought here. Say they must look for our friend when the moon is full . . .'

Hammond was too far away to overhear but he saw them talking and quickly stepped in. He took Alice roughly by the arm and Patience quickly hid the locket beneath her shawl. She watched Alice disappear inside the house, and so did Abel Corbould. His look said that he knew something had passed between them.

Eighteen

King's Mill

KING'S MILL STOOD on the banks of the Lymington River, a few miles north of the town. It had a good-sized mill pond and a huge mill wheel. When the sluice gate was opened, water from the pond surged into the mill race, turned the wheel, and inside the huge grindstones ground the wheat into flour.

Miller Sprigge, whose code name was 'the Huttite', was the last man on the list and when Edward arrived he was standing above the mill wheel in the loft doorway, where a hoist was fixed to swing the flour sacks on to carts waiting below.

'I have a message,' cried Edward. 'It concerns Tonnelier!'

Sprigge was a huge man, not just tall but as heavy and wide as the sacks he shifted so effortlessly all day long. He took a huge wooden mallet from his belt, hammered in a peg to secure the sack he was working on, then, leaving it swinging like a thief on a gallows, he disappeared inside the mill, beckoning Edward to follow.

Inside, the place was a forest of beams and timbers, and the air was so heavily laden with flour that every glimmer of sunlight became a piercing shaft in which the dust danced and sparkled. Even though the grindstones were not turning, the building seemed to tremble slightly, and as he climbed the stairs Edward felt he was inside a sleeping creature that at any moment might suddenly awaken.

At the top of the stairs there was a half-open door, through which Edward could see mountains of sacks. He pushed the door wide and as he stepped through a hand seized him by the throat and he found himself flung down on to the sacks. The miller stood over him, still clutching the mallet, and his voice was as deep as the rumble of the grindstones.

'What do you know of Tonnelier?'

'That he's dead,' said Edward, rubbing his throat, 'and that if you're the one they call the Huttite, you could be in great danger.'

*

The first villager she passed directed Patience to the mill and she rode on, past the Marl Pit Oak at full gallop, until she saw the river glinting through the trees and looked for the track that would take her down to the mill.

So determined was she not to lose her way that she never once looked behind her, which made things very easy for Sergeant Hammond, who had been following her ever since she left the house. When it became clear that she was heading for the mill, he left the main track and skirted around the pond, making sure to keep under cover, so that he could watch without being seen.

He was hoping for a clear sighting of Edward Beverley, but after Patience went inside the mill seemed deserted. Then, just as he was about to move closer, he saw a cart approaching, driven by two boys.

The cart stopped outside the mill and one of the boys whistled up at the loft door. After a moment the door opened and there stood Edward Beverley, beckoning them inside. Hammond waited for them to enter and then, with a smile of satisfaction, he turned his horse and set off to take his news to Abel Corbould.

*

Miller Sprigge was not a happy man. His mill was full of children, all of whom seemed to know more about his secret plans than he did, and one of whom was a Roundhead, daughter of the Intendant no less!

'Is it just me,' he growled, 'or does anyone else think she shouldn't be here?'

Edward was staring at the locket Patience had given him. 'What did Alice say?' he asked her. 'Is she all right?'

Patience nodded. 'Corbould has them under arrest, along with my father. But she said to "look for our friend when the moon is full".'

'Did she indeed?' The miller was beside himself. 'What else did she tell you?'

'Nothing!' said Patience. 'I don't even know what the message means!'

'Don't worry,' said Edward to the red-faced Sprigge. 'If Patience was going to betray us she'd have done it by now.'

'Well, she stays here till it's over. She can't leave!'

'I suggest we start making some plans,' said Edward. 'Tonight is the full moon and we haven't much time.' He turned to Humphrey and Pablo. 'Go back to Quincam. Tell him our friend will arrive tonight.'

Quincam was the code name of Oswald Partridge.

Edward glanced at the miller. 'I take it Quincam will know what to do?'

The miller nodded.

'Very well then, off you go,' Edward said to the boys. 'We'll stay here and wait.'

Nineteen

When the Moon is Full

IT GREW DARK. Sprigge was attending to his mill, Edward kept watch from the loft door and in the gathering gloom Patience sat waiting and tried to live up to her name. In the end she could bear it no longer.

'Do you want to tell me what's going on?' she asked.

Edward shook his head. 'I'm sorry, I can't,' he said.

'All right then, I'll tell you. You're trying to save the King. He wants to get away to France or somewhere and you're going to help him.'

Edward didn't speak, he just stared out of the

doorway. Patience hadn't been sure, but suddenly she knew she was right.

'And if Corbould catches him, he'll be locked up like my father and the whole thing will start all over again.'

Edward turned to face her. 'Not this time,' he said quietly. 'It's gone too far. If they catch him now, I think they may try to finish it.'

Patience couldn't keep the shock out of her voice. 'Kill the King? They wouldn't dare!'

'Wouldn't they?' Edward laughed bitterly. 'They killed my father and two thousand along with him at Naseby. Will they stop at one life more?'

'But, but . . . he's the King!'

Edward smiled. 'Oh, yes? And which side are you on?'

Patience bit her lip. The war had always seemed like a passing thing, it would be over soon and then everything would be back to normal. But now she saw that nothing would be normal ever again. She pushed back her red hair and stood close to Edward so that even in the gloom she could look directly into his eyes.

'You saved my life once,' she said. 'You didn't stop to ask me which side I was on then.'

'But which side *are* you on?' asked Edward.

It was a simple question but there was no simple answer.

'I'm on whichever side brings peace and lets me live my life. I'm on the side that will stop brother killing brother and sister killing sister . . .' She paused and gently touched his face with the tips of her fingers. 'I'm on your side, if you'll have me.'

Then, in the darkness of the mill, Edward kissed her and for a moment the war was a thousand miles away, until Sprigge's voice growled up the stairs.

'Horses coming! I thought you two were on watch!'

Just as suddenly they were back in the present, but Patience knew she had taken a step from which there was no turning back.

As the full moon climbed above the tree tops, three Cavaliers rode up to the door of the mill and were quickly ushered inside by the miller. From their hiding place across the mill pond, Abel Corbould and Sergeant Hammond saw them arrive, and so did ten more Levellers hidden in the forest around the mill.

Hammond was all for acting quickly, but Corbould was sure that Patience had led them to a bigger fish than Edward Beverley and now he was about to be proved right.

Inside the mill, the Cavaliers removed their

plumed hats and in the light of Sprigge's lantern the first two were revealed as the King's courtiers, the Lords Tarleton and Bressingham.

'Welcome, my lords, welcome,' said the miller. 'May I introduce Edward Beverley, here in place of the loyal Tonnelier, who met with a tragic accident . . .'

On hearing these words the third Cavalier, a smaller man, slighter than the others, stepped forward. 'Beverley? Beverley . . . don't I know that name?'

'I believe you do, Sire,' said Tarleton. 'Colonel of Horse, fell at Naseby . . .'

'Ah, yes,' said King Charles, 'most gallant, most gallant . . .'

Edward was already kneeling. 'I am his son, Sire. Your Majesty was gracious enough to appoint me High Keeper of the Forest . . .'

'Well, young Beverley,' said Tarleton, 'I hope you and the Huttite here have got a plan. His Majesty has had one or two close calls of late.'

'I believe we have, my lord.' Edward stood up and held out his hand to Patience, who stepped forward from the shadows. 'My I introduce you to a friend of mine?'

*

Ten minutes later three Cavaliers left the mill and once more mounted their horses. Now was the time for Corbould to strike. He told Hammond to take one of the troopers and arrest whoever was inside the mill while he took the others in pursuit of the King.

'Levellers, to horse!' cried Corbould, galloping forward, and on each side of the track armed troopers appeared from the forest and fell into formation behind him.

The Cavaliers had got a head start, but it wasn't long before the Roundheads began to gain ground and Lord Bressingham realized they were under attack. He shouted a warning to his companions and at the same time drew a pistol from the holster on his saddle. It was already loaded and primed but he held back, waiting for just the right moment.

Soon, through the darkness, a crossroads appeared and, while the others galloped on, Bressingham turned his horse and faced his pursuers. As soon as the Roundheads were within range, he coolly took aim and shot dead the trooper beside Corbould.

The man fell from his horse, throwing confusion into the riders behind him. One horse reared and another trooper was thrown from the saddle. Bressingham waved his hat at the milling Levellers, then spurred his horse and rode off, but along a different track from the one his companions had taken.

Immediately three troopers took off after him, which of course was exactly what Bressingham wanted.

'Leave him!' shouted Corbould.

But it was too late. Either his men didn't hear or they chose not to listen. Whatever the truth of it, the preacher found himself down to three men and the King was getting away.

'Follow me!'

Corbould put his horse to a furious gallop, but if he was afraid of losing his quarry he needn't have worried.

Lord Tarleton was actually waiting for him at the next crossroads. He had a pair of pistols and as the Levellers approached he let fly, but his aim was not as good as Bressingham's. He missed with both guns and Abel Corbould was not about to be fooled twice. When Tarleton rode off up a side track, the preacher let him go.

'Leave him,' he yelled. 'It's another trick!'

And sure enough, when the Levellers rode on they soon caught a glimpse of the King disappearing around the next bend. Corbould clenched his fist and drove the spurs into his horse's flanks. Now they had him!

This part of the forest was criss-crossed with streams and gullies and when the King realized that the enemy were upon him, he turned off the main track and tried to follow the bed of a small stream.

The stream was narrow, which made the going hard for cavalry horses. Corbould, however, was mounted on his smaller white horse and had no such problem. Leaving his men to fight their way through as best they could, he plunged on after the retreating figure until very soon the stream widened into a shallow pond, surrounded on all sides by thick bushes. The Man of Blood was trapped! There was no way out!

The King's horse reared and lunged, but it was useless. Corbould smiled in triumph, but a moment later the smile froze on his face. Although it was very dark beneath the trees, a sudden shaft of moonlight gave him a glimpse of something. He rode forward and snatched off the King's hat. A cascade of red hair tumbled free and there was Patience Heatherstone, dressed in the King's clothes and sneering at him!

'Treacherous bitch!' screamed Corbould, and with one blow of his gloved hand he struck her from her horse.

Twenty

A King's Reward

As the Levellers went off in pursuit of the Cavaliers, so the real King, led by Edward, was lowering himself into the mill race, ready to escape by way of the river.

The great wheel was silent now and Edward was just about to lead the King down to the river when a movement overhead made him stop. Sergeant Hammond and another trooper were approaching on foot, obviously intending to search the mill.

The mill race was a brick channel about eight feet deep through which, with the sluice gate closed, ran a few inches of icy water. Edward and King Charles hugged the shadows near the wall and hoped the

Roundheads would not look down. As soon as they had gone into the mill, Edward and the King went to the foot of the mill race and slipped silently into the black waters of the Lymington River.

Inside the mill, the two Levellers stood by the door, not knowing which way to move, until after a few moments Hammond became dimly aware of a staircase stretching up ahead of them. He signalled to his companion and, feeling their way like blind men, they started up through the building.

On the first floor they came upon the room where Edward and Patience had kept watch. Here the light of the full moon flooded through the loft door and Hammond found himself looking down past the mill wheel to the river where two figures were swimming out into the main stream.

Hammond let out an oath. 'Give me your pistol!' he yelled to the trooper.

The man did so and Hammond levelled it at the swimmers.

'Halt in the name of the Commonwealth!' he shouted, cocking the gun, but he never had a chance to fire. The next second he was laid low with a mighty blow from Miller Sprigge's wooden mallet.

Hammond toppled out of the loft door, bounced off the mill wheel and crashed into the darkness. His companion barely had time to draw his sword before he too was sent, senseless, to the bottom of the mill race.

Edward and King Charles heard the commotion behind them but gritted their teeth and kept swimming. The cold was merciless, but carried by the current they reached the centre of the river and soon saw on the far bank a single lantern swinging off the stern of a small boat.

'Thank God,' thought Edward, for this meant the boys had got their message to Oswald Partridge. Now he had to help the King fight against the current to avoid being swept past the boat.

With failing strength, they made a last great effort that brought them within reach of the figures who appeared from the shadows. They were hauled from the water and soon lay shivering and gasping on the small wooden jetty to which the boat was moored.

King Charles reached out his hand. 'Master Quincam, I presume?'

'The same, Sire,' said Oswald Partridge, helping the King to his feet, 'and praise God he has granted you a safe journey thus far.'

'He has, with a little help from my young friend here . . .' The King smiled at Edward.

Oswald was carrying a sackcloth bundle. 'Here you are, Master Edward,' he whispered. 'I reckon the time's as right as it will ever be.'

One of the boatmen wrapped a blanket around the King's shoulders.

'Such loyalty to our person and our cause we have not seen,' said King Charles. 'It grieves me deeply that I cannot reward such devotion.'

Edward had unwrapped the sacking to reveal his father's sword. It shone fiercely in the moonlight and so did Edward's eyes when he turned to King Charles.

'To have served Your Majesty is reward enough,' he said.

'Well said, my boy.' The King laughed. 'And yet there is one power my enemies cannot strip away. You have your sword, I see.' King Charles reached out and took it. 'Then kneel, Master Forest Keeper –' lightly he touched the sword blade first on Edward's right shoulder, then on the left – 'and arise, Sir Edward Beverley, Master of Arnwood.'

If Edward's eyes had shone before, now they positively glowed, but no sooner had the King handed back the sword than Oswald stepped forward.

'Majesty, we may miss the tide.'

'Ah, yes.' The King smiled. 'And that would never do.'

The boat was to take him to the Isle of Wight, where other friends were arranging safe passage to France. The moment His Majesty was settled in the stern, the boatmen pushed off and in two strokes they were in the middle of the river.

The King turned and called softly across the water. 'I shall send for you, Sir Edward. I need my loyal subjects beside me . . .' And with that the boat carried him into the darkness, a slight figure with all the cares of England resting on his shoulders.

'Well, Sir Edward,' said Oswald, 'we've done a good night's work. I've horses waiting. Let's get you back to Keeper's Cottage and some dry clothes.'

'I need to go back to the mill first,' said Edward. 'I promised to meet someone.'

'Did you now?' said Oswald with a smile. 'Well, the nearest bridge is in Lymington. It's going to take you a while to ride round.'

But Edward had no intention of riding. He looped the scabbard of the sword securely across his shoulders and, before Oswald could say another word, he dived cleanly into the river and struck out for the opposite bank.

Twenty-one

To the Death

SWIMMING AGAINST THE current was much harder and Edward was at the end of his strength by the time he climbed from the river. Dawn was breaking above the roof of the mill and inside there was just enough light for him to find his clothes.

'Patience!' he called as he took off the sword and began to dress. 'Patience, are you there?'

Edward looked about him and shivered. The building was silent except for the faint sound of water in the mill race, and once more it made him think of a sleeping animal.

'Master Sprigge!'

His voice seemed ridiculously loud and something

made him pick up his sword before slowly he began to climb the stairs.

The door at the top was closed, but when he gently pushed it open the first thing he saw was the miller, asleep beneath the hanging sack he had pegged the previous day. A chill breeze was blowing through the open loft door but the miller did not seem to feel it. He sat against a pile of sacks and seemed more deeply asleep than Edward would have thought possible, given the events of the night.

'Master Sprigge!'

Edward touched his arm. It was cold, icy cold, and close up the man's face had a bluish tinge. Then the miller toppled sideways and there was blood on the sacks and a bloody mess where a blade had entered his back. The loyal Huttite was not asleep, he was dead.

'Proverbs, chapter twenty-six, verse eleven. "As a dog returneth to his vomit, so a fool returneth to his folly . . ."'

Edward spun around, although he instantly knew who would be standing there. Abel Corbould, holding the dagger he had used to finish Sprigge. The preacher was smiling, enjoying himself.

'The voice of reason told me you would flee with the King. But then I thought, Edward Beverley?

Voice of reason? What am I saying? He'll come back, looking for his treacherous bitch!'

'Where is she!' said Edward.

'Ah, you know her name,' taunted Corbould, and he beckoned Edward forward. 'Come then and I will show you the punishment we reserve for those who betray us.'

Edward saw the man's eyes flicker to the door and in that moment he tried to draw his sword, but Corbould was much too quick. He was across the room in a second and, holding the dagger to the boy's throat, he wrenched the sword from his hand and threw it on the floor.

At knife point he forced Edward back down the stairs, down past the front door, deep, deep down into the growling heart of the mill, to the pit where the grindstones lay. And there they found Patience Heatherstone, still dressed in the King's clothes, bound hand and food and laid on the chute that delivered the grain into the mouth of the stones.

'What have you done to her?' asked Edward, who couldn't understand why Patience wasn't making any sound. Then he saw that a leather glove had been forced into her mouth and tied there as a gag.

Corbould threw the lever that operated the sluice

gate and Edward heard the gathering boom as water flooded into the mill race.

'Revelation, chapter seventeen,' crowed the preacher. '"What mean ye that ye beat my people to pieces and grind the faces of the poor!"'

As the words rang out, so Edward heard the churning of the mill wheel and, like a great beast coming to life, the whole building shook and trembled as the grindstones began to turn.

Corbould pulled on the rope that controlled the chute. Patience's feet lurched wildly into the air, the chute swung out over the turning stones and slowly but surely she began to slide towards the grinding pit.

Unarmed, Edward was helpless. He knew he had to get his sword and it was now or never. He aimed a frantic kick at Corbould and ran for the stairs, with the preacher two paces behind and the noise of the stones roaring in his ears.

Edward made it to the top, threw himself through the doorway and grasped the sword. But Corbould was too close and, before the boy could unsheathe the blade, the preacher had kicked it from his hand. He hurled himself at Edward, intending to finish him quickly with the dagger but Edward seized the preacher's wrist and held on for dear life, using his free hand to attempt a stranglehold.

For a moment both of them were at a standstill, strength equally matched, until, with a mighty heave, Corbould tore himself free. Edward went sprawling and the preacher reeled towards the open loft door and teetered there on the brink above the plunging mill wheel.

Almost off balance, his fingers scrabbled for the door-frame and if only he had been prepared to drop the dagger, he might have pulled himself to safety. But he would not let it go and in those vital seconds Edward's fingers found the miller's mallet and he swung wildly at the peg securing the sack of grain.

Out flew the peg and the heavy sack swung the width of the room, reaching the loft doorway at the very moment Corbould thought he had recovered.

The sack was twice as heavy as Corbould and it sent him clean through the door and into the churning mill wheel, the noise of which drowned the preacher's dying scream.

Snatching up his fallen sword, Edward half slid, half fell down the stairs, but when he reached the grinding pit he could see no sign of Patience. Was he too late?

He threw the lever that closed the sluice, but even as he did so, he knew the wheel would take far too long to slow down. Frantically he drew the sword and slashed at the rope that held the chute. It parted, the chute crashed to the floor and Patience slid out and landed at his feet.

Gently he helped her up. She threw her tied hands around his neck and, as soon as the gag was off, they kissed until the wheels stopped turning and silence returned to King's Mill.

Twenty-two
A New Beginning

ABEL CORBOULD WAS dead and the other Levellers were soon recalled to London. Mr Heatherstone told the children they could keep their treasure. Pablo and Clara could stay with them for as long as they liked, and all of them could live in the forest – all of them except Edward, that is. His plot to save the King had made him some very powerful enemies and not even the Intendant could guarantee his safety.

So a few days after the events at King's Mill, the children gathered outside the cottage to see Edward off. He was going to France, where there was talk of raising a new army to fight for the King. He had his sword, some new clothes and a fine new horse, a present from Mr Heatherstone.

'Say "thank you" for me,' he said to Patience, and then he remembered that he had a gift for her. From around his neck he took his father's crucifix. 'Will you wear it? For me . . .'

As a Puritan, Patience had never worn such a thing in all her life. She felt she was taking another step from which there was no going back.

'For you,' she said, 'yes.'

Edward slipped the chain around her neck and kissed her softly. Then he sprang into the saddle, Humphrey handed him his hat and, with all the flourish of a proper Cavalier, he bade them goodbye.

As he rode away, Patience called out to him, 'Come back to us!'

At first it seemed as though he hadn't heard, but he turned in a patch of sunlight at the very edge of the clearing.

'Of course I will!' he cried. 'I'll come back with the King!'

All the children cheered, but Alice and Patience looked at each other and in their hearts they wondered how long it would be before they saw Sir Edward Beverley again.